Little Wolf's
POSTBAG

Also by Ian Whybrow
and illustrated by Tony Ross

Little Wolf's Book of Badness
Little Wolf's Diary of Daring Deeds
Little Wolf's Haunted Hall for Small Horrors
Little Wolf, Forest Detective

First published in Great Britain by Collins in 2000
This edition specially published for World Book Day 2001
Collins is an imprint of HarperCollins*Publishers* Ltd
77-85 Fulham Palace Road, Hammersmith, London W6 8JB

The HarperCollins website address is www.fireandwater.com

1 3 5 7 9 8 6 4 2

Text copyright © Ian Whybrow 2000
Illustrations copyright © Tony Ross 2000

ISBN 0 00 711649 7

The author and illustrator assert the moral right to
be identified as author and illustrator of the work.

Printed and bound in Great Britain by
Omnia Books Limited, Glasgow

Little Wolf's
POSTBAG

Ian Whybrow
Illustrated by Tony Ross

Collins
An imprint of HarperCollinsPublishers

Dear Mr Little Wolf,

We have not met before, harrumph, but I feel I must write to you. At *Wolf Weekly* we keep getting letters from readers with problems, dash it. I am far too lupine and snappish to write back, but I have reason to believe that you are just the brute beast for the job. Sit up straight and read on, then you will find out why.

This morning, a very small wolfcub entered my office wearing a mask. He had a water pistol and informed me that he would make the papers on my desk all crinkly unless I gave him a toffee apple. Grrrumph.

This small wolfcub was wearing his sailor suit inside out, so it was a simple matter to read the name-tag on it. The name was one I think *you* know well: Smellybreff, your little brother. Pest! (Temper, you see. Snappishness. Can't help it.)

When I spoke to the small beast by his name, I suggested something that his parents might do if they found out that his hobby was

being a highwayman. The result was that he howled his head off, threw himself on his back and had a noisy tantrum. He claimed (while damaging my office floor with his head and heels) that it was all *your* fault. He claims (I quote): 'Little is always making me be a robber plus post his letters all the time. He says if I don't, he will put sauce on my ted and eat him, then make me have a bath'.

And to prove it, he pulled out a wet and somewhat chewed envelope from his pocket.

Thanks to Smellybreff's dribble, the gum on the envelope had lost its grip. My curiosity was aroused and I was unable to resist opening the letter and reading it.

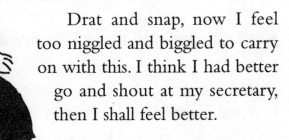

Drat and snap, now I feel too niggled and biggled to carry on with this. I think I had better go and shout at my secretary, then I shall feel better.

Yours suddenly,

Peevish Wolfson the 3rd (Ed)

Bah! Are you still there Little Wolf?

Where was I? Ah yes. Look, I hate praising, but bite me black and blue if that letter of yours wasn't a masterpiece! It was one you wrote to your parents who have their lair near the River Rover in Murkshire. You asked them to come and take your baby brother back, though not in so many words. You *suggested* that if they have their 'darling little baby pet' tucked up with them this winter, they will save loads of cash on hot water bottles. I must admit that was brilliantly put. Crunch and gnash it! Sadly, however, to judge by my brief meeting with the ghastly Smellybreff, I suspect that they still prefer *you* to look after him.

You went on to mention in your letter that Smellybreff is in the habit of stealing your stamp collection and sticking it all over himself.

You tell your parents, 'It might be a good idea if you posted him to a nice far-off bunnyburger restaurant. There, he could be much happier everafter than staying with me in a big draughty old house in Frettnin Forest.'

Another very nice try. It showed imagination and – more importantly – *craftiness*!

Most of *Wolf Weekly*'s readers are just as spoilt, sad and hopeless as your brother, grrrumph. They are always writing to the magazine with their problems. Nitwits! So I need an Agony Aunt who can write back with crafty and cunning ways to keep the moaners happy.

Hurry and let me know if *you* will take the job for a large salary.

I am, young sir, reluctantly yours,

Peevish Wolfson the 3rd (Ed)

Not any more

HAUNTED HALL SCHOOL

FRETTNIN FOREST BEASTSHIRE
HEADS: LITTLE WOLF AND YELLER WOLF ESQS
DEPUTY HEAD: SMELLYBREFF WOLF ESQ
CARETAKER: STUBBS CROW ARKSQWIRE

Dear Yeller,

You are a very funny tricker. Go on, that was *you* just saying you are Mister Editor of *Wolf Weekly* saying have a job. Go on, own up! You nearly made me fall for it 2, because the writing was all posh, not like your normal loud and hilly words.

But I knew it was you at the end part, when you said have a large celery. Because you know I like crunchy snacks, but you did the spelling wrong, har har!

So go on, own up, who helped you?

Was it Stubbs, or Normus maybe?

Yours gotyoubackly,

Littly

PS What did you think of my frog-
in-the-box? Did you like him
jumping out and going squirt with
pond water in your eye? Good eh?
I trained him spesh for that.

MY ROOM
YORE OWSE
FRETTNIN FORIST
BEESTYSHEAR

DEAR LBW,

TA A LOT FOR THE FROGGY, YUM YUM, TASTY. BY THE WAY WHAT JOB? ALSO, WHAT IS AN EDITOR, DO YOU MEAN HEAD HITTER?

BECUZ I AM WUN OF THOSE, YOU CAN SEE THAT FROM MY TRICK RUBBER HAMMER ON A STRING WOT I SENT WIV THIS LETTER.

SO HEE HA HACK,
GOT YOU BACK!!

FROM YORE BEST FRIEND AND CUZ
WITH NOBS ON AND NO RETURNS,

YELLER

PS I HAVE ASKED NORMUS AND
STUBBS AND THEY SAID BEARS
AND CROWCHICKS DON'T DO
WRITY TRICKS BECUZ 2 HARD FOR
THEIR BRANES.

Not any more

HAUNTED HALL SCHOOL

FRETTNIN FOREST, BEASTSHIRE
HEADS: LITTLE WOLF AND YELLER WOLF ESQS
DEPUTY HEAD: SMELLYBREFF WOLF ESQ
CARETAKER: STUBBS CROW ARKSQWIRE

Dear Peevish Wolfson the somethingth,

I did not write back quick, sorry. I thought you were just my best friend and cuz Yeller doing wun of his tricks on me.

So um, yes, if you want, I will be your letter answerer to your *Wolf Weekly* readers.

I like doing writing but not being an Agony *Aunt*. Because I have got a faymus dead uncle called Bigbad, have you heard of him? He died of the jumping beanbangs and became ghost and star attraction at our school Haunted Hall. So best if I can be an Agony *Nephew* instead.

Also, I like celery but will you pay me a large bag of gold instead? (I have lost all mine.)

Yours hintingly,

Mister Helpful (Get it?)

PS I am Little Wolf really, but in ~~dizgizz~~ ~~desgoise~~ just pretending for your Problem Page in Wolf Weekly.

Dear Little Wolf,

Thank you (achh, I hate having to say that). Anyway, what I just said for agreeing to work for me. All those little pests moaning on were starting to set my teeth on edge. But you have obviously had plenty of practice in dealing with moaners like your baby brother and your splendid arch-criminal uncle, Bigbad Wolf.

It pains me to admit it, bah, but I like the name Mister Helpful. It is a fine disguising name, or, as they say in French, a *nom de plume.*

Now you had better make a start at agony answering. I am enclosing a hopeless letter from a fearfully sad young wolverine. You are to deal with it. This is a test. If you succeed, you shall have gold. If you fail, I shall send you a tape-recording of me going 'Bah, young cubs today are useless! Not like me, when I was a young chaser. They always let you down!' etcetera etcetera.

Yours doubtingly,

Peevish Wolfson the 3rd (Ed)

enc

Ma Belle Maison Splendide,
Dogood Way,
Near Windy Ridge,
Beastshire

Dear Wolf Weekly,

I love your magazine, especially fur and fitness tips. But what tips can you give for cubsitting? I am starting my first job as a

sitter soon, and I fear baby wolfies can be difficult. Is loving care enough?

Yours anxiously,

Prudence Wolf (Miss)

Not any more

HAUNTED HALL SCHOOL

FRETTNIN FOREST, BEASTSHIRE
HEADS: LITTLE WOLF AND YELLER WOLF ESQS
DEPUTY HEAD: SMELLYBREFF WOLF ESQ
CARETAKER: STUBBS CROW ARKSQWIRE

Dear Mister Wolfson,

You remind me of Uncle, making me do tests and saying Or Else. How do you spell nat? Is there a 'g' in it? (Cannot find room for wun.)

Any gold coming my way, hint hint?

Yours testedly,

L Bad Wolf the wunth

From the Sharp Pencil of Mister Helpful ~
Wolf Weekly's Agony Nephew

Dear Miss Prudence,

Shame about you having such simple dimp ideas. But never mind, I have done you tips in a poem so even a ~~ngt ngat~~ nat could learn them just by humming them over and over.

Wolfcubsitting for Beginners

If baby is a problem
And you don't know what to do,
Give him something fun to play with,
Like a nice big pot of glue.

Tip 2 for the baby wolfie is,
If he goes wah wah,
Take him out for fish and chips,
Or let him drive your car.

If wolfie keeps on crying,
Sit down in your chair,
Give him a pair of scissors
And let him cut your hair.

If baby wets his nicknocks,
The best thing you can do,
So he will not get all upset
Is wet your nicknocks 2.

Wun last tip for beginners is,
(You will find this helps a lot),
Let the baby watch the telly,
Then you can have a nice long
zizz in his cot.

Yours tippingly,

MR Helpful

Dear LW,

You are hired. You
know how much it
irritates me to say
excellent, so I won't.
I will say Tish, Tosh and
Grrrumph instead, and
you will just have to
work out what I really
think and accept this
medium-size bag of
gold. Carry on with
work of this quality
and I shall be forced,
rrreluctantly, to send
you an even larger one.

Now hurry up, write yourself an announcement so that readers will be expecting you. Go on, get on with it. I shall print it on the Sports Page.

I remain yours hatefully with a capital Harrr,

Peevish Wolfson the 3rd (Ed)

BOTTLED GHOST OF BIGBAD WOLF STILL MISSING: FOX SUSPECTED.

… AND THERE IS still no sign of the missing ghost of ex-Criminal and Terror, Bigbad Wolf. He was formerly headmaster of Frettnin Forest's Cunning College, and later, School Spirit and Resident Horror of Haunted Hall. Our reporter has learnt that the whisky bottle in which he made his grave on account of its label 'Powerful Spirit' has been stolen. The number 1 suspect remains Mister Twister, Foxy Crook and Master of Disguises, but his whereabouts are unknown.

BEAVER ARRESTED FOR SWEARING

FRETTNIN FOREST POLICE were last night questioning a beaver who was very rude after a sliding incident on the banks of the River Riggly. Asked by PC Thick where he lived, he answered, 'A big dam'.

WOLVES MAKE A MEAL OF BUNNY WANDERERS IN CUP SEMI-FINAL

IT WAS SPILLS, thrills and cooking skills all the way at the Howl Lane ground today. The home team just gobbled up the opposition.

In just 35 seconds, the Wanderers were in the net. They were in the pot after just one minute and served up with carrots and boiled potatoes well before half time. With the entire opposition off the field, Wolves were able to shoot at will but they could only be bothered to score three goals each.

Commenting later, team coach Terry Grab said: 'All credit to the Wanderers. They had some very tasty and seasoned players. I thought their goalie was really hot.'

Final score:
Wolves 99
Wanderers 0

CALLING ALL READERS!

Arrrroooo!

CALLING ALL READERS of Wolf Weakly Weekly. Guess who is going to be your new problem page Agony Nephew? Me. I am Little Wolf really but you must pretend not knowing and say Dear Mister Helpful if you want to get a reply printed all poshly in this faymus mag. Because Mister Helpful is my nom de prune (French).

So go on, what is up with you? Write quick.

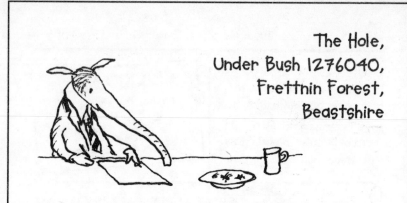

The Hole,
Under Bush 1276040,
Frettnin Forest,
Beastshire

Dear Little— woops sorry I mean, Mister Helpful,

I feel starving all the time, even just after dinner and tea. What can I do about it?

Yours probingly,

Antony Anteater

Dear Antony,

Y not get a bigger hanky and try doing xtra hard parps in it?

If your nose is still blocked up, try a chimney sweep. Also, here is a good tip. If your friends say 'Let us go round the anthill and have a good blowout', that means suck really, so careful in case of going in reverse.

Yours *bong appetitely* (meaning enjoy your grubs, French),

Monsieur Helpful

PS You could try picking more. But not at parties, a bit rude, hem hem.

27

The Compost Heap
Up the messy end of Bodger Badger's garden
The Set
Spooke
Grimshire

Dear Mister Helpful,

My Dad makes me feel really really
small all the time. He says things
like, 'You will never make
anything of yourself, only a
crunchy snack'.

My dream is to
be the best xylophone player in Beastshire. I
have got the arms and legs for it, don't you
think?

Please be encouraging.

Yours crawlily,

Milly Pede

Dear Milly,

About being a crunchy snack or a xylophone
player. That is a hard wun. Your best thing is, go
round to my Dad's lair and say, 'Hello Mr Wolf,
Mr Helpful says can I play *God Save the Queen*
on your toothies?' You will soon find out
which wun you are best at.

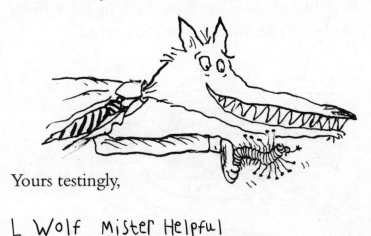

Yours testingly,

L Wolf Mister Helpful

The Lair
Lonesome Mountain
River Rover North
Murkshire

Dear Son,

I know it is you being Mister Helpful. You cannot fool me, I am your mother. Trust you to let down our family reputation for wicked selfishness and badness. You have always been a bit of a goodun, I fear. I 'spect your Uncle Bigbad's ghost is turning over in his whisky bottle if he knows what you are up to.

But, did you send a pesky millipede round to cheek your father? **Well done!** That was a bit more wolfish. It made him go raving mad with fangache. He had to go to the dentist and do you know what he found? A mini xylophone plus two bong-sticks stuck in his hollow tooth! **Good one!**

So your reward is that you can look after our darling baby pet Smellybreff for a bit longer. Remember, give him everything he whines for. It is the only way.

Love,

Mum

PS Make sure this pic gets in your posh mag, I had it taken spesh.

Bodger Badger's Garage
The Set
Spooke
Grimshire

Hello,

The thing is, oo-ar, Oy was rootlin' about at the top of my garden last week, when Oy heard be-ootiful music come a-tinklin' from moy compost heap. Blow me down if it wasn't a teeny little bug a-playin' on one of them there xylophone things. Fantarstic it was.

Yippee! Oy am a bit a bit slow on the uptake, but Oy have just had a fantarstic idea! Oy reckon Oy shall make a fortune chargin' folks to come and have a listen! Then Oy shall buy meself a chicken farm and give up garage work. Now, moy problem is, Oy can't make up me moind, should Oy start counting me chickens yet?

Yours oo-arrly,

Bodger Badger

Dear Bodger,

Umm, no, probly not, sorry. My dad has scoffed your music player.

But if you are keen on a nice change from garage work, I will give a tip 2 you. Take your glasses off 1st. Glue some feathers on your spanners, then hold out some corn saying, 'Here chicky chicky'.

Yours nevermindly,

Mr Helpful

The Grassy End,
Yellowsmoke Swamplands
Grimshire

Dear Mister Help,

I am a teenage leopard but I have got no spots
at all. I feel so ashamed. What can I do?

Yours embarrassedly,

**Whizz Fleetfoot (age 2 but don't forget to
times by 7, OK?)**

Dear Whizzy,

Keep eating loads of greasy food plus sweeties, chips and all stuff like that. If still no spots, find a hole in a wall and move in. Put up a notice outside saying HANSUM LARGE WEASUL, then everyone will go, 'Cor he has got big mussuls for a rodent'.

Yours adequately,

Mister Helpful

37

The Smellery,
Quite a bit away from everyone else,
Frettnin Forest,
Beastshire

Dear Mr Hurtful,

Sometimes I get so lonely. Would it help if I changed my perfume? Please be frank, my best friends will not tell me.

Yours defensively,

Irma Skunk

SMELL THIS SAMPLE

PS I am spraying you a small sample on this letter.

From the Sharp Pencil of Mister Helpful ~
Wolf Weekly's Agony Nephew

Dear Irma,

Pew! Dank you for da dample
dat you dent. How long before
I can take the peg off my
doze?!!

I hab passed your
letter on to Wiffer
Warthog, The Hogwallow,
Muckheap on Sea.

You 2 will be a happy couple together I bet.
Plead do not bodder to wride and dank me.

Yours gassedly,

Mister Fainting

39

The Nest
Twiggly Junction
Big Elm

Watcher Matey,

My old Cock Sparrer and me are not feelin' our normal chirpy selves. We have got problems with our new fledgie, just 2 weeks out of his egg.

I am not sayin' he is fat. But put it this way, feedin' him his grubs is like tryin' to load a cement mixer with a teaspoon. Also he takes up all the nest already. Plus his voice is a bit funny. He never seems to say 'cheep' or 'tweet' like our other babies dun. He just seems to get the hiccups sort of. We are worried about what he will be when he grows up.

Yours down in the beakly,

Mrs Hazel Edge-Sparrer

Dear Mrs Sparrer,

Never mind if your fat fledgie is
a hopeless flier and tweeter.
Just teach him to count up
to 12 and pop him in a
clock. (Must be Swiss and
do not forget to put him
on a bit of elastic.) Then
he will have a nice job
for life.

Yours guessingly,

I M Helpful Esq

PS Does he go cook and oo a lot?
I bet he does.

41

The Filthy Mantled Pool,
Yellowsmoke Swamplands

Dear Mister H,

Let me just yelp that I need some help
And I need it in a hurry.

I ain't no liar my throat's on fire
And my mouth is kinda furry.

Get me off the hook, come and take a look,
'Cos you're a real nice kind of chappy

Pop along today with a soothing spray
And Mister, make it snappy.

Yours saying Ahly,

Al R Gator

Dear Al,

Have we met before? Is your middle name Rap? I think it is and wun time you swallowed a small cub listening to his Walkwolf, yes? Anyway, thank you for your letter, it was quite catchy. Sad about your sore throat. In a way, hem hem.

I am a bit 2 busy to jump in your mouth today. Your best bet is hang a very large sign saying OPTICIAN on your snout. If you are very lucky, maybe a shortsighted doctor will pop in for an eye test.

Or if you know any piglets with water pistols, maybe you could throw them a bottle of gargle and say, 'Hoy you smellies, I bet you can't squirt the little dangly thing up the dark end of my gob with this'.

Tempting, eh?

Yours soothingly,

Mister Helpful

THE PILE OF LEAVES
THE HEDGE
NEAR THE BIG BEECH TREE THAT GOES EEK
IN A STRONG WIND.

DEAR MISTER HELPFUL,

When I was younger, I had lots of fun playing football but not any more, I cannot even touch my toes. These days I am feeling so flat, I do not know what has come over me. Can you recommend a pick-me-up?

Yours low downly,

SPIKY HEDGEHOG

Dear Spiky,

You say you do not know what has come over you. Did it go 'Brrrm Brrm Beep'? If it did, your best pick-me-up is probly a shovel. Or, if not, Y not tumble dry yourself. Jump in the tumble-dryer wunce a week and that way you will soon be rolling over and over like washing. After, if you are still a bit rubbish at kicking and heading, never mind, you can be the football.

Yours sportingly,

Mister Helpful

Dear Mister,

I do not know how I shall ever hold my chin above water again. My tail just fell off. What shall I do? I feel so unattractive.

Yours pointlessly,

Newton Newt

Dear Newton,

Newts' tails are all damp and horrible anyway.

My best advice is, forget it. Just do a hop and a skip, saying:

I am so luckee,
My tail fell off todee,
So now there is less of me,
To get all cold and clammy!
Hip hip hoorah times 3!

PS You can buy blue stuff down the shop for sticking up posters and tails, it is called Newtack. But as I say, Y bother?

49

Dear Mister Helpful,

On behalf of all the dear creatures of Frettnin Forest who have benefited recently by your magnificent advice, allow me to express our sincere gratitude.

Please come round to my enormous mansion and collect a luxury hamper of succulent food. Although I am of huge richness, I am but a weak and helpless widow.

I am sending you a picture of me in my old lady's nightie and glasses and everything. Sad to say, therefore, I will be unable to leave my bed and hand it to you personally. Instead, I shall leave it for you in a safe place in a big black sack at the bottom of a deep pit in my garden.

Feel free to pop down and collect it any time. Can you advise me when to expect you?

Your devoted fan,

Miss ER Wittert

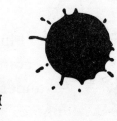

Dear Mister Twister,

What a twisty letter you sended. I know you are not really Miss ER Wittert. That was just a mixup of your real name, yes?

But I knew it was you. Because clue number 1 was your foxy paper made me sneeze by its peppery smell.

Plus Clue 2 was your tail coming out peepingly from under the bedclothes in the photo.

Plus clue 3, you left a red whisker sticking to the stamp.

You say can I advise you? Answer yes, here I go. Can you see my pic A of a piece of string?

Now can you see pic B?.

It is the same string as pic A only with knots in. Good, because now you must copy pic B, ready steddy go.

Now you have got knotted, har har.

Yours unfooledly,

Guess who?

PS I know who pinched the whisky bottle with Uncle Bigbad's powerful spirit in. You. Give him back now, or else.

Bathing Towel House
Scouting Lane,
Roaring River,
Murkshire.
CUB 3RD

Dear Mr Helpful,

I am trying to locate a wolf cub by the name of Little. He is an honorary member of my pack, the 3rd Murkshire. Can you assist, please?

I met him last summer in Beastshire, on the shores of Lake Lemming in Frettnin Forest, where I had taken my Cub Scout troop on a camping trip. He stayed with us for quite a while and achieved a great deal for a small furry animal.

He gained his Navigator and Explorer Badges and he took particular pride in the special Cub Scout Adventure Award (1st Class) with certificate and badge that we awarded him. And we were over the moon  to have him in our pack. Because, as I said to him then, 'sonny jim, you have made our visit to Frettnin Forest something special. You are the first real wolf cub we have met'.

My patrol leaders, Sanjay and Dave, never stop talking about Little Wolf. He was such a cheery, plucky young chappy. This year, we are looking forward to a jamboree, a big gathering of all the Cub Scouts in Murkshire and Beastshire. We have picked the perfect spot for it – Spring Valley, just by the bend in the Spring River, South-East of Lonesome Woods. Smashing tent country!

My problem is this. There has been a lot of talk lately that Spring Valley is haunted. They say that ever since he went bang, the ghost of the dreadful Bigbad Wolf wanders about in the woods and forests shocking innocent wanderers, with his great big horrible red eyes and his great big horrible yellow teeth. All nonsense I dare say. But because of the rumours, I can hardly get enough cubs together to fill one tent, let alone make up a proper Jamboree. Most disappointing.

You would be doing a very good deed if you could put me in touch with Little Wolf. If he (and perhaps some of his friends) would join us, I feel certain that it would encourage some of the faint-hearted chappies to change their minds and come camping!

Yours DYB DOB DYBly

Jim Toggle (Akela)

Dear Mr Toggle,

Lucky you wrote to me, because I know all about L Wolf Esq. Also about his cheery pluck and young chappyness, thank you hem hem. I let him have a read of your letter and he has sent you 1 back.

Your gooddeedly,

Mister Helpful

HAUNTED HALL SCHOOL

Dear Akela,

Arrrroooo! from me (Little Wolf) to you, also Sanjay and Dave.

Mr Helpful says you want to get some cubs together for camping near Lonesome Woods. Good, because camping used to be my worst thing, now I love it kiss kiss.

I will bring my best friend and cuz Yeller. He is loudest with the best ideas, plus a fine tricker. Next is Stubbs, only a crowchick but he has got a clever beak plus

he does good loop the loops. Normus Bear is my newest chum. He does not fly (no wings) and his ideas are rubbish but he is already a cub, also tuff and likes daring deeds.

They all say ARRRRROOOOOOOOOO! to jamborees!

Plus do not fret and frown, we have got a plan for getting you loads more to be in your pack. So bring plenty of tents. See you in Spring Valley.

Yours surprisingly,

LBW

PS I will have to bring my baby bruv Smellybreff. He is Ok in a way, but best not teach him lighting fires, eh?

PPS me, Yeller, Stubbs, Normus and Smells have made a detective pack called Yelloweyes Detective Agency. We have not detected anything yet BUT (big but) maybe we will detect my lost Uncle Bigbad in Spring Valley, yes?

CALLING ALL READERS!

Arrrroooooo!

Stop being wurrid. Come and be in a cubscout pack instead with Little Wolf, Smellybreff, Yeller, Stubbs and Normus and do jamboreeing in Spring Valley.

We will have campfires, singsongs, widegames, badgework, choclit fingers, adventures, potty noodles, alphabetti spaghetti and SPESHLY humshuss and scrumshuss bakebeans, hmm yessss!!

I *was* Mister Helpful, but I am fed up of being Agony Nephew now. It gives you arm-ache and not enuff muckabouting. Plus, Mr Peevish Wolfson says:

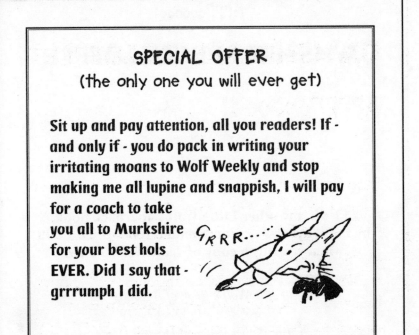

SPECIAL OFFER
(the only one you will ever get)

Sit up and pay attention, all you readers! If - and only if - you do pack in writing your irritating moans to Wolf Weekly and stop making me all lupine and snappish, I will pay for a coach to take you all to Murkshire for your best hols EVER. Did I say that - grrrumph I did.

GRRR......

So change WURRY to HURRY and LET'S JAMBOREEEEEE!

Arrrrrrrrrooooooo!

Yours ridingalongonthecrestofawavely,

Little Wolf

Arrrooooo!

WHSmith SPECIAL OFFER

**£1 off any other Little Wolf paperback book,
by Ian Whybrow - recommended retail price £3.99 -
when you buy a copy of *Little Wolf's Postbag*.**

Little Wolf's Book of Badness
ISBN 0-00-675160-1 £3.99 rrp

Little Wolf's Diary of Daring Deeds
ISBN 0-00-675252-7 £3.99 rrp

Little Wolf's Haunted Hall for Small Horrors
ISBN 0-00-675337-X £3.99 rrp

Little Wolf, Forest Detective
ISBN 0-00-675452-X £3.99 rrp

**£1 off any of the above. Present this voucher
at the till when making your purchase.**

- - - - - - - - - - - - - -✂- -✂- - - - - - - - - - -

Terms and Conditions

*1. This voucher entitles you to £1 when you purchase a Little Wolf
 book by Ian Whybrow, in paperback, from* WHSmith
2. Offer exclusive to WHSmith *High Street stores*
3. Voucher valid until 31.8.01
4. Cannot be exchanged for cash or any other merchandise
5. Only 1 voucher per purchase
6. May not be combined with any other offer
7. Subject to availability
8. Only original unaltered vouchers will be accepted

WHSmith barcode

0001 2645